SNOOP!
YOUR COMPLETE DETECTIVE KIT

By Debra Mostow Zakarin
Illustrated by Carrie Abel
Cover illustration by Margaret A. Hartelius

Special thanks to Active Concepts, Inc. for many of the mystery kit components and to CPC Food Service for the Argo Cornstarch packaged with this book.

CONTENTS

I SPY!

Ever wondered who ate every cookie in the house, or who left the TV on all night long? Ever wanted to send a secret message to your friend—that no one else would be able to read? Well then, this is your lucky day!

Whether you need to snoop, like to snoop, or just want to snoop, **SNOOP!** will teach you all you need to know, and it comes with everything you need to conduct your own investigations:

- Use the **magnifying glass** to help uncover clues and to read the Snoop Secrets hidden throughout the book.
- Use the **ink pad** and **finger-print I.D. cards** for collecting fingerprints.
- Use the **fingerprint powder** and **feather** to dust and identify fingerprints you find.
- Use the **invisible ink** and **magic decoder pens** to transmit top secret information—or use one of the **code machines** at the back of the book.

Of course, the more you snoop, the more you'll want to add to your kit. Here are just a few things a super snooper should have on hand:

- A **notebook** for recording clues, taking notes, and storing secret codes.
- A **flashlight** for finding clues in the dark.
- **Plastic baggies** for collecting evidence.
- **Clear adhesive tape** for lifting fingerprints.
- **Gloves** for keeping your own fingerprints away from the evidence.

Remember, too, that you don't have to snoop alone. You'll cover twice as much ground with a partner on the case!

CASE 1 USING SNOOP SKILLS

You've had a long day at school and you can't wait to get home and grab those chocolate chip cookies that have been calling your name since before lunch.

You throw down your book bag and head for the kitchen. Yikes! The cookie jar is empty! You're determined to get to the bottom of this mystery. But how?

Snoop Secret: Keep a notebook handy for recording observations.

1. Case the Joint

Look around the kitchen. Is anything out of place or different? Is anything missing (besides the cookies!)? Did the cookie culprit leave any clues behind?

Be careful not to touch anything until you're sure it's not some kind of clue. And leave the scene exactly as you found it. Take notes on everything you see.

You notice that a cabinet door is open. You investigate and find a plate is missing. *Aha!*

2. Now Think

The biggest job of any snoop is to answer these questions: Where? When? How? Why? and Who?

When you think about this case, it looks like the guilty party has fled the scene with a plate full of cookies. But where would someone *go*?

3. Search for Clues

You try the family room. The TV is still warm, and the sofa cushions are dented and covered with crumbs. Someone was here . . . and whoever it was sure was a slob! You taste the crumbs. Sure enough—chocolate chip!

You look over at the coffee table and find an empty plate . . . and a crumpled napkin. You observe the napkin more closely. What do you see? Lipstick, perhaps? Yes, neon orange— the same yucky color that your older sister always wears!

4. Weigh the Evidence

The evidence is strong. Only your sister could make such a mess *and* wear such a gross shade of lipstick. You confront her with your findings. She confesses and promises to make it up to you.

Pat yourself on the back because you've just cracked your first case using your most important snoop skill—observation! But being a careful observer takes practice. Here are some exercises to help you sharpen your skills:

- Sit in a room with a friend for three minutes and just observe. Each of you should write down everything you hear, smell, see, and feel. After three minutes, exchange your lists. Are they the same? What did you observe that your friend didn't? What did your friend observe that you missed?

- At home after school one day, write down everything you can remember about your classroom. What posters are on the walls? How many desks are there? Who sits where? The next day, bring the list to school and compare what's actually there to what you wrote down.

- Look at the picture below for one minute. Then cover the picture and answer the questions at the bottom of the page. How did you do?

Questions

- What is the name of the detective agency? *Snoop*
- How many kids are wearing glasses? *1*
- Name four things found on the desk. *pencil, notebook, lamp, telephone*

- What time is it? *12:25*
- How many times does the word "Snoop" appear? *6*
- Name four things hanging on the wall. *clock, hat, coat, diploma*

5

CASE 2 FINDING FINGERPRINTS

It's very early on a Saturday morning and you're the first one up. But what are those voices coming from the family room? You investigate.

You find no one in the family room, but the TV set is on and very warm. Looks like somebody forgot to turn it off last night. But who?

You spot an empty glass on the floor and get down to observe it more closely. Are there any lipstick marks on it? Not this time. Your sister was spending the night at a friend's house anyway. No problem. There's still a good chance the glass can tell you who the guilty party is. How? From fingerprints!

What are fingerprints?

Fingerprints are one of the best methods around for making a positive identification. Basically, they are the marks left on objects by the oil and sweat on the ridges of your fingertips. When your fingertip touches a smooth surface, the ridges leave behind a distinct pattern that only you can make.

Snoop Secret: Why do you have ridges on your fingers? They help you grip and hold onto things.

Fingerprint Facts

- No two people in the whole wide world have the same fingerprints—even identical twins.

- Fingerprints get bigger as you grow, but the patterns stay the same.

- Your palms and lips and even the soles of your feet leave behind unique patterns, too. That's why babies have their footprints recorded right after they are born—for identification.

- Fingerprints cannot be changed. Even if you remove the top layer of skin, fingerprints will grow back exactly the same way.

- Animals have unique prints, too. Monkeys and apes have fingerprints. Dogs have nose and paw prints. And horses have distinctive prints on the calluses, or "chestnuts," on the insides of their legs.

There are three kinds of fingerprints that detectives work with:

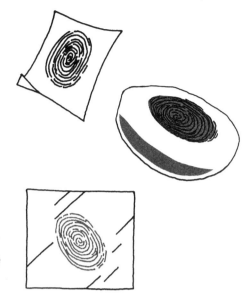

Visible – These are marks you can see, left by things like dirt, food, or ink.

Plastic – These are marks you can see and even feel because they make an indentation in things like mud and clay.

Latent – These are marks you can't always see, left by the sweat and oil on the ridges of your fingertips.

Fingerprint experts classify fingerprints into four groups:

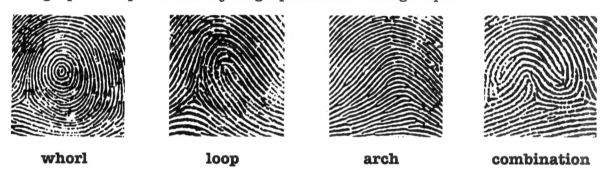

| **whorl** | **loop** | **arch** | **combination** |

What kind of fingerprints do you have? Use your magnifying glass to examine the tips of your own fingers.

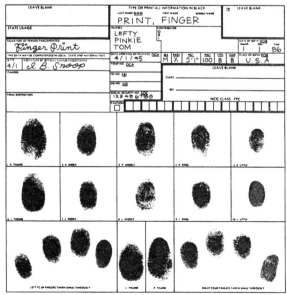

Today, thousands of people are identified each month by their fingerprints alone, and not just criminals. Fingerprints can also be used to locate missing persons and identify people with amnesia who can't remember who they are.

In order to identify the fingerprints they find, detectives must have fingerprints on file to compare them to. The Federal Bureau of Investigation (FBI) has over 2 billion sets of fingerprints on file on cards just like this one.

You can start your own file, too. Begin by recording your own fingerprints....

RECORDING FINGERPRINTS

You will need:

ink pad

paper

fingerprint I.D. card (page 21)

1. Make sure your hands are clean and dry, then cut out one of the fingerprint I.D. cards on page 21.

2. Press your fingertip onto the ink pad, rolling smoothly from left to right. Your fingertip should be covered in ink.

3. Practice making fingerprints a few times by pressing your inky fingertip onto a piece of paper.

4. Now see how the boxes on the I.D. card are labeled for each finger? Get your finger inky again and press it onto the correct box, rolling again from left to right so that your whole fingerprint is transferred. (Be careful not to roll back again, though, or you'll smudge your print.)

5. Repeat for each finger and thumb of each hand.

index

Complete your fingerprint file by taking prints of everyone you know—or think you might suspect! To make identification easier, classify the prints as whorl, loop, arch, or combination, and keep them grouped by type.

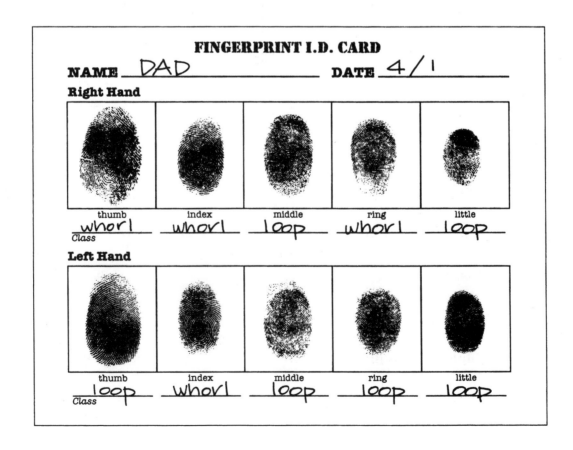

FINGERPRINT I.D. CARD

NAME **DAD**   DATE **4/1**

Right Hand

thumb	index	middle	ring	little
whorl	whorl	loop	whorl	loop

Class

Left Hand

thumb	index	middle	ring	little
loop	whorl	loop	loop	loop

Class

Snoop Secret: Don't forget to wash your hands when you're done, or you'll be leaving fingerprint records all over the place!

8

Fingerprints are just one type of "physical evidence" that detectives look at. The FBI has reference files on everything from shoe prints to animal hair, natural and synthetic fibers, tire treads, and even automobile paint. Are there any other reference files you'd like to collect?

Fingerprint Firsts

A.D. 700: Thumbprints are used to sign business contracts in China.

1300: Thumbprints are used to stamp government documents in Persia.

1883: Great Britain's Sir Francis Galton publishes *Fingerprints*, describing the first scientific method for classifying prints.

1891: Argentina becomes the first country to set up fingerprint files to identify criminals.

1904: New York City's police department becomes the first in the U.S. to fingerprint everyone arrested.

1924: The FBI Identification Division begins collecting fingerprints from all over the U.S.

1994: The FBI receives over 34,000 fingerprint cards a day.

DUSTING FOR FINGERPRINTS

But what about that glass you found beside the couch...?

There's a very good chance that the person who left the TV on is the same person who left the glass on the floor. And there's an even better chance that the person who left the glass on the floor left his or her fingerprints on the glass. But latent prints like these are invisible. How do you make them visible? Easy..."dust" them!

You will need:

fingerprint powder

feather

magnifying glass

fingerprint file

gloves (optional)*

1. Lightly scatter a little of the fingerprint powder on the part of the glass where fingerprints are likely to be—like the middle, where you usually pick it up.

2. Use the fluffiest part of the feather to gently brush away the excess powder. Dust back and forth as lightly as you can, until you start to see the fingerprints come through. The powder will stick only to the oily marks left by the finger ridges.

3. Keep brushing until every detail of the print is clear. (Just be careful not to brush the print away!) Then blow away any extra powder.

4. Use your magnifying glass to observe the fingerprints more closely. Now you can compare these prints to those in your fingerprint file.

*In order not to smudge the prints or mix your own prints with them, it's a good idea to wear gloves while you dust. But if you don't have gloves handy, don't worry. Just be careful to touch only the edges of the glass.

Snoop Secret: To make latent prints show up better, shine a flashlight at them from different angles.

Snoop Secret: Don't worry if you run out of fingerprint powder. Ordinary cornstarch will also work.

LIFTING FINGERPRINTS

But what if your fingerprint file isn't handy? Then you'll have to keep the prints and take them back to headquarters with you. But how? Easy..."lift" them!

For this you will also need:

clear adhesive tape

black paper or board

(You can also use the back cover of this book.)

1. Tear off a piece of clear tape big enough to cover the dusted print.

2. Place the tape carefully over the print.

3. Gently lift up the tape (the print will lift up with it) and stick it onto the black surface.

4. Always label this and any other evidence with the date, the location, and your initials.

5. Now you can take the prints with you back to headquarters and use your magnifying glass to compare them to the prints in your fingerprint file.

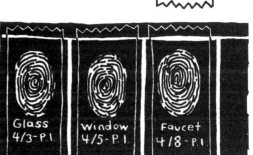

A-ha! A perfect match! You've found the culprit and Case 2 is solved! You're really on your way to becoming a super snooper!

Top Five Places to Find Fingerprints

1. Mirrors
2. Windows
3. Drinking glasses
4. Faucets
5. Doorknobs

Can you think of other good places to find fingerprints?

CASE 3 SENDING SECRETS

You're in the middle of silent reading period and you have a very urgent, top secret message to relay to your best friend. There's just one problem....No talking in class! What can you do? Pass a note? Maybe. But what if the note falls into the wrong hands?

This is exactly why secret codes and ciphers were invented.

- A **code** is made by replacing letters or words with signs or symbols.

- A **cipher** (say "sigh-fur") is made by rearranging or changing each letter in each word.

To anyone who doesn't know your code or cipher, your message will look like gobbledegook. But to you and your friend, the meaning will be crystal clear.

CIPHERS

Making a cipher can be as easy as rearranging letters. See if you can figure out these top secret messages:

Backward

.TCEPSUS RUO HCTAM YEHT .STNIRP EHT DEKCEHC I

Answer: I checked the prints. They match our suspect.

Rebroken

LE TSCR AC KTH ISC ASEB YLU N CH

Answer: Let's crack this case by lunch.

Up and Down

E N H L O O T O C U S
B O T E O K U F R L E

Answer: Be on the lookout for clues.

To make your ciphers even trickier, try combining them, using random capital letters, or not using any punctuation at all. The message below is backward and rebroken. Can you read it?

GN IHTY NAREH PIC EDNA CUOYSI HTRE HPICE DNACU OYFI

Answer: If you can decipher this, you can decipher anything.

Caesar's Alphabet

Substituting letters is another way of ciphering. Over two thousand years ago, the Roman emperor Julius Caesar invented a special cipher for sending secret messages to his friends. He replaced each letter with the letter three places to the right in the alphabet: **A** was **D**, **B** was **E**, **C** was **F**, and so on.

Snoop Code Key

| regular alphabet: | A B C D E F G H I J K L M N O P Q R S T U V W X Y Z |
| cipher alphabet: | D E F G H I J K L M N O P Q R S T U V W X Y Z A B C |

Can you decipher the message below by using the key to look up the regular alphabet letters that each cipher letter stands for?

L WKLQN VKH'V RQ WR XV

Answer: I think she's on to us.

Cipher Wheel

Some snoops use machines such as cipher wheels to help them substitute letters. Cipher wheels are great because you can carry them with you so you don't have to write down or memorize code keys. Ask a grown-up to help you make cipher wheels for you and your partner.

You will need:

> **scissors**
>
> **cipher wheels** (page 23)
>
> **brad fasteners**

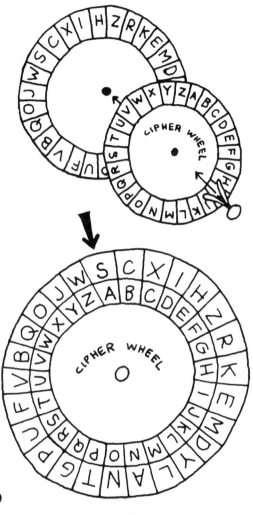

1. Cut out the cipher wheels on page 23.

2. Place the smaller wheel in the center of the larger wheel: The inner wheel will be the regular alphabet; the outer wheel will be the cipher alphabet.

3. Punch a hole in the middle of the wheels and insert the brad.

4. To use the cipher wheel, pick a "key" letter on the outer wheel. It can be any letter you like—say **S**. Turn your wheel until the key letter **S** matches up with the letter **A** on the inner wheel.

5. To write a cipher message, substitute the cipher letters on the outer wheel for the regular letters on the inner wheel. In other words, if your key letter is **S**, and your message is this...

   WE'RE BEING FOLLOWED

   ...your cipher message would be this...

   QH'PH CHEAR ZNYYNQHI   (Key Letter: S)

   (Be sure to write down the key letter, too.)

6. To uncipher a message, just line up the key letter on the outer wheel with the letter **A** on the inner wheel. Then look for the cipher letters in the message on the outer wheel and write down the matching letters that appear on the inner wheel.

Can you use your cipher wheel to figure out this message?

DA YMSANIV QOX XO DVOZ KOIS YOHAS   (Key Letter: M)

Number Cipher

You can substitute numbers for each letter, too.

Snoop Code Key

A	B	C	D	E	F	G	H	I	J	K	L	M	N	O	P	Q	R	S	T	U	V	W	X	Y	Z
26	25	24	23	22	21	20	19	18	17	16	15	14	13	12	11	10	9	8	7	6	5	4	3	2	1

Can you figure out this message?

23.22.8.7.9.12.2.   7.19.18.8.   14.22.8.8.26.20.22.
26.21.7.22.9.   9.22.26.23.18.13.20.

Answer: Destroy this message after reading.

Pigpen Cipher

For this cipher, a pattern of lines and dots is substituted for each letter.

1. Draw two tic-tac-toe boxes and two large **X**'s, like this:

2. Draw dots inside the second tic-tac-toe box and **X**, like this:

 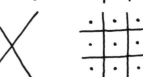

3. Fill in the letters of the alphabet like this to make your Snoop Code Key:

Snoop Code Key

A B C D E F G H I J K L M N O P Q R S T U V W X Y Z

⌟⌴⌞⌝⬝⌜⏋⏌⏉V⟨∧⟩⌟⌴⌞⌝⬝⌜⏋⏌⏉V⟨∧⟩

Can you read this message?

V⏉⌴⌝⏋⌜⏋?

Answer: Whodunit?

Snoop Cipher

Feel free to make up your own personal Snoop Code Key by substituting any shape or symbol for each letter of the alphabet. You can even use musical notes.

Snoop Code Key

A B C D E F G H I J K L M N O P Q R S T U V W X Y Z

♩ ♩. ♪ ♫ ♩ ♩. ♪ ♩ ♪ o ● ◉ ● P P♮ P♪ ♪ P P♪ ♪ 𝄞 𝄢 ♭ # ♮ —

Now write your own Snoop code key here:

Snoop Code Key

A B C D E F G H I J K L M N O P Q R S T U V W X Y Z

‒ ∠ \ ⟂ X ⊥ ( ) ⟩ □ △ ▨ ⇶ ⫽ ∭ ▽ ≡ ⫿ ⊠ ▨ ⊞ ⊙ ⋅ ▨ E K

14

HOW TO CRACK A SECRET CIPHER

Working undercover, you intercept what looks like a cipher—but you can't find a key in your own codebook that works. Can you still try to decipher it? Sure! All it takes is a little common sense, and a little knowledge of the English language:

1. Look for the symbol that shows up most often. Since the most commonly used letter in the English language is **E**, there's a good chance that the most common symbol stands for **E**. (**T** is the second most commonly used letter, then **A**, then **O**, then **N**, then **R**.)

2. The most commonly used double letter combinations are **LL**, **EE**, **OO**, **TT**, and **FF**. If you see a double symbol combination, it probably stands for one of these.

3. The most commonly used words are **THE**, **OF**, **AND**, **TO**, **IN**, **A**, **IS**, **THAT**, **FOR**, and **IT**. If you see certain groups of symbols reappearing, they probably stand for one of these words.

4. **T** is the most commonly used letter at the beginning of a word. A symbol that shows up at the beginning of several words could be a **T**.

5. **E** is the most commonly used letter at the end of a word. If you see a symbol at the end of lots of words, it might be an **E**.

6. If there's a symbol that appears by itself in the message, it probably stands for an **A** or an **I**.

Now that you know the secrets to cracking ciphers, can you read the message above?

Answer: To Snoop or not to Snoop

CODES

Your best friend is sleeping over, but it's lights out and Dad says to keep quiet. Still, you and your friend have loads of important information to exchange. What do you do?

Flashlight Code

One answer is to use a flashlight. Make up a code in which different flashes mean different things. For example:

TWO FLASHES – code for "Stop laughing!"

THREE FLASHES – code for "Let's sneak into the kitchen."

LIGHT ON CEILING – code for "Someone's coming!"

LIGHT MOVING IN CIRCLES – code for "I'm still not tired!"

Morse Code

Of course, you could also use Morse code. Morse code was invented by Samuel Morse as a way of transmitting messages by telegraph (which, by the way, Morse also invented).

Morse code is made up of combinations of dots and dashes which stand for different letters of the alphabet. Dots (•) stand for clicks or taps followed by short rests. Dashes (—) stand for clicks or taps followed by long rests. Two long rests follow each letter.

A •—	**E** •	**I** ••	**N** —•	**S** •••	**W** •——
B —•••	**F** ••—•	**J** •———	**O** ———	**T** —	**X** —••—
C —•—•	**G** ——•	**K** —•—	**P** •——•	**U** ••—	**Y** —•——
D —••	**H** ••••	**L** •—••	**Q** ——•—	**V** •••—	**Z** ——••
		M ——	**R** •—•		

Morse code can be sent all kinds of ways. Use a flashlight (use short, one-second flashes for dots, and long, two-second flashes for dashes, and pause two seconds between each letter) or tap on a desk. In a crowded room, you can even blink Morse code to your partner.

Super Snoop Code

Codes have been used to relay secret information for hundreds of years. The military still uses them to refer to secret projects and missions. Do you remember "Desert Storm"? This was the code name for the U.S. Army's military operation in the Persian Gulf.

Even the president has a code name! Do you know the code names of these presidents?

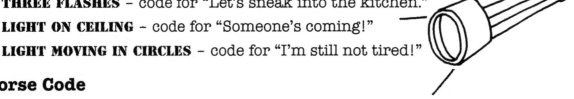

John F. Kennedy	**Ronald Reagan**	**George Bush**	**Bill Clinton**

Answers: Lancer   Rawhide   Timberwolf   Eagle

By substituting special words for other words or ideas, you can make up your very own snoop code. For example, if this were your Snoop Code Key:

PRINCE CHARMING - code name for your partner

DANCE - code word for "come over"

MIDNIGHT - code word for "school"

GORILLA - code word for "sister"

KISS - code word for "spy on"

CASTLE - code word for "house"

And you wrote this:

**PRINCE CHARMING
DANCE TO MY CASTLE AFTER MIDNIGHT SO WE CAN KISS MY GORILLA**

It would mean this:

**(PARTNER'S NAME)
COME OVER TO MY HOUSE AFTER SCHOOL SO WE CAN SPY ON MY SISTER**

Of course, no matter how good your snoop code is, your cover would be blown if you signed your own name to top secret documents! That's why all good snoops need their own official code names (or numbers), too.

Snoop Codebook

You've devised hundreds of codes. Now you just need to keep track of them. Here's how:

- Make a special book for all your Snoop Code Keys.
- Make a copy of your codebook for your partner, too.
- Keep your codebook in a safe, secure location.
- Disguise your codebook to fool other spies.
- Make a dummy codebook to fool other spies.
- Change your codes from time to time.

Did you know sailors used to bind their secret codebooks in lead so that if their ship were ever captured, they could toss the codebook overboard and know that it would sink all the way to the bottom—safely out of enemy hands?

TRANSMISSION

No matter how tricky your codes and ciphers are, you can never be too careful. Transmitting messages is risky business.

The ancient Greeks had their own clever ways of disguising secret messages. During one war, a Greek ruler shaved his messenger's head and then tattooed his message on it. When the messenger's hair grew back, he was sent to deliver the message. The ruler knew that if his enemies found the messenger and searched him, they would find nothing. But when the messenger arrived safely at his destination, his head was shaved again and the message was revealed!

Of course, not all messengers are as willing to be shaved and tattooed. In that case, here are some other ideas.

Scytale

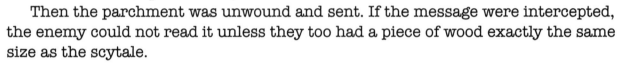

The scytale (say "see-TALL-ee") was another Greek invention—a piece of wood around which a long strip of parchment was wrapped. A message was then written across the parchment, like this:

Then the parchment was unwound and sent. If the message were intercepted, the enemy could not read it unless they too had a piece of wood exactly the same size as the scytale.

You can easily make your own scytale.

You will need:

two identical pencils or pens
(one for you and one for your partner)

lined notebook paper

scissors

tape

1. Cut a long, thin strip of paper by cutting along the notebook lines.

2. Wrap the strip tightly around your pencil or pen. (If your message is a long one, tape two strips together.) Fasten each end to the "scytale" with a piece of tape.

3. Write your message in a line across the paper. If you need to, add more lines.

4. Remove the tape and unwrap the paper. Then fold it up and send it to your partner.

5. To read the message, all your partner has to do is rewrap the strip around their own pencil or pen.

Snoop Grid

A snoop grid is another speedy way of sending top secret information.

You will need:

snoop grids (page 23)

scissors

hole punch

paper

pencil

1. Cut out the snoop grids on page 23.

2. Use the hole punch to cut out the dark circles in the grids.

3. Keep one grid for yourself and give one to your partner.

4. To record your message, place your grid on a piece of paper. Trace around the corners to show exactly where the grid goes.

5. Now write out your message, letter by letter, in the open spaces. (Note: Your message must be less than 60 letters long.)

6. When those spaces are filled, turn the grid a quarter of a turn and continue filling in the spaces. Keep turning and filling in until your message is complete.

7. Remove the grid and fill in any blank spaces with random letters.

8. Send the message to your partner.

9. To decode, place the grid back over the message and write down each letter as it appears. Turn the grid a quarter of a turn until you've gone all the way around and revealed the entire message.

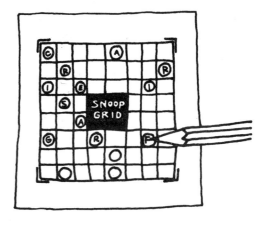

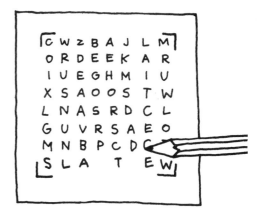

Invisible Ink

Make extra sure that only your partner can decode your message by using the special invisible ink and decoder pens that come with this book.

- Simply write out your message in invisible ink and pass it on to your partner. No one else will even know there's a message written there! When your partner colors over it with the decoder pen, the secret message will magically appear.

- You can also write a phony message in real ink on a piece of paper, and then write your secret message in between the lines in invisible ink.

- Another sneaky way to use invisible ink is to write part of every letter in your message in regular ink (black ink works best) and the rest in invisible ink, so that it looks more like a bunch of random lines than real writing. When your partner colors over the visible lines with the decoder pen, the complete letters will instantly appear.

- Or plan a super secret treasure hunt for your partner! Make up some clues that will lead your partner from place to place and write them down in invisible ink. Leave a new clue waiting by the answer to the last clue to make a treasure trail, ending with the "treasure" (maybe a brand-new code device!). Not only will your partner have to figure out the clues, she or he will have to use the decoder pen to read them in the first place!

Smuggling Secrets

Think of unusual places to hide your messages, where no one else would guess to look. For example, who would ever suspect a chewing gum wrapper of containing top secret information?

Or how about a book or magazine? Find a page that has all the words or letters that you need for your message. Mark them with tiny dots, then mark the page and send it on to your partner. To decode, your partner simply writes down each word or letter with a dot next to it.

Can you figure out this message?

Answer: Happy Snooping!

20

FINGERPRINT I.D. CARD

NAME _____ **DATE** _____

Right Hand

thumb	index	middle	ring	little

Class _____

Left Hand

thumb	index	middle	ring	little

Class _____

FINGERPRINT I.D. CARD

NAME _____ **DATE** _____

Right Hand

thumb	index	middle	ring	little

Class _____

Left Hand

thumb	index	middle	ring	little

Class _____

FINGERPRINT I.D. CARD

NAME _____ **DATE** _____

Right Hand

thumb	index	middle	ring	little

Class _____

Left Hand

thumb	index	middle	ring	little

Class _____

FINGERPRINT I.D. CARD

NAME _____ **DATE** _____

Right Hand

thumb	index	middle	ring	little

Class _____

Left Hand

thumb	index	middle	ring	little

Class _____